THE DREAM OF ALCESTIS

ALSO BY THEODORE MORRISON

THE DEVIOUS WAY

TRANSLATED AND EDITED BY THEODORE MORRISON

THE PORTABLE CHAUCER

THE DREAM
OF ALCESTIS

THEODORE MORRISON

ILLUSTRATED BY MARVIN BILECK

NEW YORK · 1950

THE VIKING PRESS

SET IN CALEDONIA AND GOUDY OPEN TYPES

AND PRINTED IN U. S. A. BY HADDON CRAFTSMEN

TO

K. J. M.

THE DREAM OF ALCESTIS

I

In Thessaly the stricken king, Admetus,
Vexed with an illness no one understood,
Lay on his couch. The friend of Hercules
And husband of Alcestis, weak and flushed,
Picked at the troubled air with his fine hands
And frowned and wet his thin lips fretfully.
Servants had carried king and couch as one
Into an open courtyard of the palace,

Where on his delicate skin the fever glistened
Under the autumn sun.
                              "This oracle
That you have sent for, quite without my leave,
What if I should reject it?" said the king.

   The priest, Apollodorus, heard his threat
Almost as if he welcomed it. "Take care,
Admetus. When the gods adopt a word
Its own force executes its hidden portent."

   "Why dread the oracle?" Eugenius asked.
"The gods may send us favorable word.
It may presage your health again, Admetus,
For some propitiatory act, perhaps,
Or some appropriate sacrifice."

                              The priest
Turned from the king to the old counselor
And said with a stiff irony, his eyes
Pursed up unblinking under their flat brows,
"You speak like any man of policy,
But policy is nothing to the gods.
The gods approve piety first of all.
Impiety is the first crime they punish."

   Admetus raised himself. His elbow struggled;

The peak of his broad shoulder was forced up
Until it touched his neck. Eugenius helped,
Bracing his back with pillows till his head
Came upright on his spine, and his blond beard,
In which each hair gleamed with a separate luster,
Opened around the word "Impiety!"
As if it were a morsel of spoiled shellfish
He found it necessary to spit out.
He sat a moment gathering strength from anger,
The blue pulse of his temples throbbing hard,
His eyes lit with fastidious contempt.
Over his knees the embroidered coverlet
Made purple hills with needlework of snow.
He raised an arm that let the veins be seen
Through the white flesh inside the well-turned wrist.
   "The king is guilty of impiety,
Therefore the gods have punished him with sickness.
I know the charge, and I despise it, priest!
I have more piety beneath the nail
Of my least finger than all priests rolled in one.
What is my piety, and what is yours?
Mine is toward reason, and whatever author
Reason may have that lies beyond our reason.

Yours is toward violence, you men of blood,
Butchers of bullocks, murderers of sheep
In your religious barbecues! I know
The method in your piety. You need
Two vices for your business, guilt and fear,
And you have learned where they may both be found
And stirred up to your purpose. Ignorance,
That is the spring you tap: ignorance.
You tell the mob, 'The gods have been offended,
The gods must be appeased.' Fear seizes them.
Their sins rise in their throats, and in blind guilt
They howl for victims. With your bloody knives
You dabble in the necks of rams and heifers
And say, 'See there, the blood has drained your guilt;
The gods are satisfied.' You throne yourselves
On every throttled lust. Well if it stops
With beasts as victims, and not man himself."

Shocked and aggrieved, Eugenius lifted up
His aged wrists, imploring, "Be advised!
As I have been your friend, your father's friend
These many years, this dread impolitic word
Goes round the court, this word impiety.
It blows suspicion up and down the kingdom,

And foolish apprehension. Foolish, I say,
And yet as there are gods, and as they rule us—"

   "You palter with the truth; you take his side,"
The king accused him. The old man stood embarrassed.

   "We have sent a runner to the Delphic shrine.
He has been gone these seven days already,"
Said Apollodorus. "If the god is pleased
To let his word be known, shall we proclaim it,
Or will you hear it first in private audience?"

   "Bring me the mischief when you have it, priest,"
Admetus answered. "Some equivocation
Contrived by your malignant cunning, doubtless.
Bring it to me; let's find what reason can do
To offset superstition."

                              The priest went out,
And the king said, "The man's no man at all.
He's a kind of rigid, bifurcated serpent.
He has a snake's eye. Every time he speaks
I look for the forked flicker of his tongue.
His policy is forked, his mind is forked.
What else can you expect of superstition?
But I forget. He has no more belief
In the nostrums that he peddles than quack doctors

Who know the filth their poultices are made of."
   Eugenius gave a sigh of long-tried patience.
   "Our popular religion, true enough,
Is a rich soil for myth, and well-manured
For superstition. Yet impiety
Is real, though much belief is not. This word
The god will send us through his oracle,
You won't deny—"

           "What god? What oracle?
These priests grow oracles in their dark minds
Like mushrooms in the muck of unlit caves,
And bring them out to pander to the craving
That feeds on riddles. Tell me, Eugenius,
Have you ever seen a god?"

                "No."

                   "No, of course.
You have not seen nor have I seen a god.
Old women see them in the dusk, like dogs
Who bark at shadows in a vacant room.
The crack-brained peasants who have only sheep
To talk with on the wild and lonely hills,
They see the wand of Mercury beneath
The cloak of every stranger at a crossroads.

· 8 ·

Believe me, I am not so impious
To think that underneath this natural world
There may not be—there is, no doubt—some mind
That holds the wide seas in its lap, and lays
The universal stonework under reason.
But all these popular gods who rape and revel
And stud the earth with their miraculous children
And send diseases down to punish us
For spite or jealousy, they debauch us more
Than drugs or drink."

             "I am not so bold in thought
As you, Admetus. Rational, I hope,
As a man and Greek may be; but yet I think
There is more in the world than we can understand
By reason alone."

            "Don't take me for a fool
Until you must," the king said irritably.
"As if I thought my petty fund of reason
Could pocket up the universe, explain
Why hair grows on my head, or to what end
We live and breed and die, or why the sun
Resting its chin on the horizon's edge
Looks twice as big as when it's twice as hot

· 9 ·

Up there in the zenith! We float on mystery,
And the wise man knows it better than the fool.
But having said as much, most men forget
What they have said, forget that mystery
Is just what they have called it. They go on,
When they have granted the unfathomable,
To pitch their petty plumblines overboard
And fathom it. They fathom it with gods
And demigods and ghosts and what you will,
Notions and fantasies that lust and fear
And hate send up out of our ignorance.
Fear needs tabu, and so invents a god
To say 'Tabu!' This is the way we turn
Our mysteries into dogmas. Thus we prop
Our worst beliefs by saying 'We do not know.'
See how these priests will take some common chance,
My illness, or some odd coincidence,
And bring the gods down on my quiet house
To threaten us with blind catastrophe
Unless we appease, propitiate, and grovel!"

   "I cannot rule your thoughts; you are the king,"
Eugenius said. "But as your minister,
I would say, consider policy, Admetus.

You have given yourself a license with your talk
That spilled in casual ears would wreck your kingdom.
You have already flushed one pair of ears
With words that I'm afraid will turn to venom."
    "The venom of the priests is mine already.
They poison all my people's minds against me.
Their rumors and their hints crawl in and out
Like snakes that chill men's testicles with fear.
Priests have one policy: to keep their power.
They are the rival kings in every kingdom.
The anointed sovereign must not grow too great,
And they have ways of keeping him in check.
Their game with me is that old superstition,
An ailing ruler means an ailing realm.
You know: the king coughs, and the next step is
The cows will have abortions; after that
The crops will fail, the springs dry up, the wives
Turn barren and their husbands impotent.
The gods have been offended, none knows how,
But they must be appeased; and what that means
Is necks for the pontifical knives to cut.
Oxen may be enough, or not enough.
Sometimes a human victim is required.

Perhaps all strangers and barbarians,
All who are tainted as unlike ourselves
And live by other customs, must be flogged
Or killed or driven in exile over the borders.
I fear this oracle, Eugenius.
I apprehend no good. But I am sick.
I cannot counter them."

                         The king fell back,
Lay on the couch like a man drained of life,
And his eyes closed. The angry energy
That had sustained his thought collapsed and failed
When he had given it words. Eugenius
Bent anxiously above his fluttering breath.
Admetus opened his eyes again and smiled.

   "The day has taxed your strength," Eugenius said.
"Shall I call the queen? She can redeem it for you."

   "Not now. We must have a policy at once.
Put your wits on it."

                         "Forgive me if I wonder
Whether you know how great is the advantage
Your throne has in Alcestis. Why, she's fit
For any court in Greece! I can only say
Auspicious was the star that led you to her."

"It was a good star, if you call it that."

"She's a great lady, and the mother of children,
And yet she seems a girl, still in the blossom."

The king smiled. "Your affection for the queen
Is well known, and her great respect for you."

"Ah, yes. I see what you imply. Respect!
I talk like an old man doting on a girl.
Don't be afraid. If I were young again,
You would do well to post your royal spies
About my chamber, just to keep your throne
From walking off some night and your queen with it.
But I am harmless now."

                    The king said kindly,
"You have been young these eighty years and more."

Eugenius wagged his beard. "I'm a cracked wineskin.
My liquor is fast running out."

                    A voice
Discreetly begged their recognition; turning,
They saw between the columns of the door
Bion, the poet, his youth curled on his head
In ringlets, and his lyre beneath his arm.

"The king is indisposed," Eugenius told him.
"He cannot hear your ode."

Bion said suavely,
"I had no thought of troubling him at present.
The queen has news, and I am sent to ask
Whether your counsels may be interrupted."

The king's face blanched a little. "Have the priests
Finished their business? Are they ready for us
Before we are for them? Tell her," he said,
"That she is welcome."

Bion bowed his leave.

"Ready or not, we'll hear them," said the king.

Then at the door, between the slender columns,
The beauty and the girlhood of the queen
Appeared, and smiling at Eugenius,
Quickly she crossed the court until she stood
In white and gold above the purple couch.

"Which is it now, sickroom or council room?"

"A little of both. We're plotting ways and means
To counteract our priests, who grow too zealous.
I thought, perhaps, news of their oracle
Had come to you."

"What oracle is that?"

"If I were stronger," said the king, "I'd match them!
But here I lie, day after day, my mind

As clear as ever, or so at least I think,
But all the world grown faint and far away,
Nothing that I can grip on in this fever.
It's just as though some sleight of hand had twitched
Half the reality of nature from me."

"You think too much about yourself, Admetus.
You ought to see the children every day
And watch your horses and your hounds awhile."

"What, watch the paces of a horse from bed
And know I cannot ride?"

                              "The queen's advice
Is wiser than you know," Eugenius urged him.
"Health is contagious no less than disease.
Try it, and you will find how salutary
The company of simple, natural creatures,
Children or animals, can be. Or athletes,
Moving so lithe and young, relaxed and loose
Until the moment comes for wound-up effort,
And then the winner scores a victory
Cleaner than battle, though akin to battle,
With a perfect heave or a scuttle to the finish
In which the formal and the free are blended.
There's health in watching them!"

The king said shortly,
"Everyone has advice for an invalid.
What is your news, Alcestis?"

                              "Don't be frightened.
We have a guest, a formidable guest."

   "A guest? Well, there are gods, I see it now,
And they take pleasure in tormenting me.
Who but a god would lay it down, Eugenius,
That hospitality is the first of duties
And send me guests when I am sick and helpless?"

   "Wait till you hear," the queen admonished him.
   "Well then, who is it?"

                              "Hercules is with us."
   The king threw off the linen coverlet
And struggled to get up, but with light hands
Alcestis held him back. "Don't try," she said.
"He knows that you are sick; he's all concern.
We've coached him tactfully. He's being washed,
And after he's eaten up an ox or two
He'll pay his compliments."

                              The king relaxed
And his beard parted briefly in a smile.
"With Hercules I feel like a timid boy

Afraid his rough big brother will pick him up
Between his thumb and finger and crack his ribs.
And all that vast simplicity of his skull!
That's the real danger in him, and the kindness,
Whichever happens to come uppermost."

"His friendship is a great strength to your throne,"
Eugenius said.

"True. We should turn this visit
To our advantage somehow. It comes pat.
Hercules is a god, as people say,
Or half a god. We've half a god in the house!
He has the status of a hero now,
And when he dies everyone will believe
He's gone to join the immortals on Olympus.
Our priests can't sniff at that."

"First," said the queen,
"While he is feasting, let your father and mother
Come in and make their little daily visit."

"I can't be spared?" Admetus asked. "Not once?"

"Give them their little pleasure. Let them come.
It breaks the day for them only to see you
And ask you how you are."

"And let me know

At great length how they are, and tell me again
Their petty grievances."

                    "They're very old,
Your father and mother."

                         "Bring them in, Alcestis."
She left them, and the king said, "Think, Eugenius.
We have not met our problem. I can tell
By all the omens a man's hackles whisper
The priests have nearly ripened their design.
Their oracle is pecking at its shell."

Eugenius paced a slow turn back and forth,
His hands behind his back, but he was silent.
Then at the door Alcestis reappeared,
Bringing the aged parents of Admetus.
She led them toward the couch, keeping slow time
With their infirmity.

                  "How are you, mother?"
"How are you, son? I'm afraid that you're no better,
So flushed and hot. You ought to eat more fruit
And drink more goat's milk."

                       "How are you today,
Father?"

              "What, boy?"

"I said, I hope you're well?"
The old man put a finger to his ear
And bent it forward. She who had been his queen
And had become his spokesman answered for him.
"He can't sleep, that's the worst part of his trouble.
The cooks can't do his food the way he likes it.
They just can't seem to make it appetizing."

Hoarsely the old man said, "That poet fellow,
Bion, I think his name is, he just told me
That Hercules is here. That so?"

                                 "Yes, father."

"I'd like to see him. I'd rather have seen Jason.
He was the skipper of the Argonauts.
But Hercules or any of the heroes
Would be a sight to take down to the grave.
I'd like to see the lion that he killed
In the forest of Cithaeron. I've heard tell
He always wears the skin around his neck."

Alcestis smiled. "You hunted with the best,
Didn't you, father?"

                   The old man said with spirit,
"Admetus couldn't pull a bow with me.
Too lazy."

"I looked on hunting as a pastime,
Not a career," the king said. "All the same,
I used to get my boar when I was active.
Remember the one I killed—"

His voice broke off.
The others took the lead from his changed glance.
They turned, and in the doorway stood a man
Who shrank the little court as if a stage
Where some divinity play blundered along
Had suddenly for a visiting star received
One of the gods in person. Bearded and scruffed
With heavy scrolls of hair glinting with oil,
His head was like a trophy over which
Hunters might wrangle, and distinguished him
As male adult of some prodigious species.
His cheeks puffed up beneath tremendous sockets
Where large eyes glittered white, and the black pupils
Peered out as if the intellect of a child
Were orphaned in a house too great to fill.
Fresh from his beef and bath, his oiled limbs glistened.
His knees moved with a feline suppleness,
And down his back the legendary pelt,
The lion of Cithaeron, lightly hung.

"Welcome to Thessaly," proclaimed the king
And tried again to rise, but Hercules,
Advancing with stiff courtesy, beamed at him
And raised a quelling hand. "Lie down, lie down.
I know you're sick, they told me so outside.
Just pay me no attention," said the hero,
The drum-roll of his voice beating the walls
With cavernous heartiness.

                    "Forgive me, then,"
Admetus answered. "You are one of us.
My mother and father, Hercules."

                        The hero
Bowed to their silent curiosity.
"I honor the mother and father of my host.
And you, Alcestis, lady, beautiful queen.
If only I had a thousand of my labors
To do for you, they'd all be easy work."

  "I never had a prettier speech than that,"
Alcestis smiled.

               "Eugenius, if you will,
Pull up the divans, let these people sit,"
Admetus asked.

             They formed into a group

Balanced on one side by the royal couch
And the king's face wrinkled in a fine amusement,
And on the other side by Hercules.

"This is a place I always like to come,"
The hero said. "It isn't like Mycenae.
Down there, you know, they're all afraid of me,
Won't even let me live inside the town.
They think I'll tear the palace up, I guess.
You people here, you don't seem to be scared.
You treat me like an equal."

                        "May I ask,"
The king inquired, "to what we owe your visit?"

   "That what you'd like to hear about? My cousin,
You know him, King Eurystheus, in Mycenae,
The one who thinks up jobs for me to do,
Though I can't blow my nose inside his palace,
He's taken a fancy to some mares he's heard of
Owned by King Diomedes up in Thrace.
If what they tell about them is the truth,
They ate a stable boy. Man-eating mares!
I'm on my way to Thrace. I'll just drop in
On Diomedes, but I won't be welcome
As much as here in Thessaly, I guess."

He chuckled genially, and the queen said,
"What vicious animals! Men must have beat them
And used them cruelly to turn a mare
Into a monster."

                       "How will you drive them home,"
Admetus asked, "from Thrace back to Mycenae?"
   "Oh, legwork, just another piece of legwork.
March, bivouac, and march, that's all it means.
I have a way with animals, you know.
The gods have never yet produced a monster
I can't lead like a lapdog on a string
Unless I kill it. The Hydra, that was one,
And the big boar up on Mount Erymanthus,
And then the stag that had the golden horns,
The stag of Artemis. I killed them all
Or captured them, just as Eurystheus wanted."
   "I'd like to see that lion," said the king's father.
"I'd like to feel the hide."

                       Hercules rose,
Unfastened the pelt obligingly, and said,
"Take it, look at it all you want. Good skin,
Well tanned, in prime condition."

                         The old man seized

And fingered it with infirm eagerness.

   "The jobs I like best are the ones that call
For tracking down a monster. Some I've had—
Well, the less said the better. Cleaning out
The stables of Augeus, there's a case!
Twelve thousand head of stock, and not a fork
Used in a dozen years." He pinched his nose.
"I found there was a river ran nearby,
Dug it a new bed, swung it through the stables,
And that was that."

                    "Your exploits are a theme
For all the bards in Greece," Eugenius told him.

   "Now, as I understand it," said the king,
"These tasks of yours come from the gods themselves,
Eurystheus acting only as their agent."

   Hercules frowned; his geniality
Passed through a cloud. Some inward thought or image
Darkened his face and forced through his great chest
A rough, constricted breath.

                    "It doesn't matter,"
Alcestis said, "whether it be the gods
Who give the word for all your famous labors
Or King Eurystheus as a mortal man.

Giving your strength to what you have to do,
That's all that matters."

                              "Just what I say myself,"
The hero answered, beaming with relief
At a hard question lifted from his mind.
"I never stop to ask who gives the orders.
I take the jobs. If it weren't King Eurystheus
It would be someone else. The oracle,
The one at Delphi, told me I must work,
Do any task that's set for me to do.
That's the one way I can wash out my crime,
In the sweat of work. I guess it's all I'm fit for.
Without a job, I don't know why it is,
I'm apt to kill someone before I know it."

   He brooded for a moment, then with a laugh
That might have chilled a man who trusted less
In mind for safety than the king, he said,
"It's best to kill a fellow now and then
In the regular way of business, if you have to.
If I've learned one thing, then I've learned that much.
Suppose I'm doing a job, and someone's killed.
It's not considered crime. No one gets bothered,
And there's no retri— what's the word I mean?"

"Retribution, perhaps?" the king suggested.

"One of those words the priests use," said the hero.

"But tell me, Hercules," the king persisted,
"The Delphic oracle is a god's voice,
Wouldn't you say it is?"

"Well, naturally.
Delphi is the oracle of Apollo."

Eugenius interposed. "A messenger,"
He said uneasily, "has been dispatched
By the priests of Apollo here in our own court
To the oracle at Delphi. As you see,
We are troubled by the sickness of our king.
I think Admetus wants to talk with you
About these matters, knowing that you yourself
Are thought to be divine in origin."

He shot the king a glance of admonition
And rubbed his palms together nervously.

The hero gave him a prodigious wink.
"Some people take me for a demigod,
That's true enough. I am my mother's son,
But some say King Amphytrion was my father
And some say it was father Jove himself."

"Lovely Alcmena," said Alcestis gently.

"She was no more beautiful than you, Alcestis,
Though I say it of my mother."

                              "But you yourself,"
Admetus asked, "which tale do you believe?
Do you consider yourself the son of Jove
Or do you call yourself Amphytrion's issue?"

   The hero, saved twice from his questioner,
Looked from Alcestis to Eugenius
For help again, but each face in return
Stared at him pale and silent. Passion gathered
Under his ribs, and his vast torso labored.
It broke forth in a child's bewildered wail,
Save that it stunned them with a deep male roar.

   "Ask my dead wife, my slaughtered Deianeira,
My children that I killed with my own hands!"

   His knees flexed, and he bounded from the divan
To hang above them like an apparition
Seen on the forked front of a thunderhead.
His arms made rending motions in the air
As if he would have torn the roots of trees,
But it was flesh and bone that he was tearing,
Strewing the blood and hair about the court
In a compulsive mimicry of the act

He had committed and was still committing
In the theater of his skull. "My Deianeira,
My children, torn as if Actaeon's hounds
Had hunted them! All dead, all dead and gone.
Would I have done it," he begged them, with his eyes
Abject for pity, "unless I had been mad?
Yes, madness, that was it. Hera was jealous
Because Jove, like as spit to King Amphytrion,
Lay with my mother all the livelong night.
She sent the madness on me. It was vengeance.
That's why I have to work and do my labors,
That's why the oracle commanded me
Work, work the crime out, work with your hands.
And yet I'm half a god—me, Hercules!"

   "Never was hero's tale that I've heard tell
Without a crime or two," said the king's father.
"I've had hot blood myself, times that I've known."

   Alcestis put her hand on the old man's arm
And hushed him. "There's a divinity," she said,
"In common strength well used."

                                        Hercules thanked her,
More certain of her kindness than her meaning.
"Well, I'll be off. I'll have to get to Thrace

Before the snow flies. If I stayed around
No telling what I might do next. I'll go."

   "If we can be of service," the king said,
"A skin of wine to take along the road,
Provision of any sort—"

                     "No need at all.
Perhaps I'll stop again on my way back,
Driving those mares. There won't be much to graze;
They'll need some fodder."

                       "My stables will be ready,
And while you fatten your man-eating mares,
We'll hope to give you better comfort here."
Admetus raised a deprecating hand.

   "Well, now, I'm sorry if I've been a trouble.
Short stay and come again, that's a good rule.
Where is my lion skin?"

                  "I shot a lion,"
Said the king's father, holding up the pelt.
"Right through the heart, first arrow."

                        "He could hunt,"
Said the king's mother. "It seems like yesterday
No man in Thessaly could tire him out.
He'd ride till we had to lift him from the saddle.

We're eighty, now."

                        "One thing I'd like to know,"
The old man asked. "What did you shoot him with?
I've looked, and I can't find a weapon mark."

  "I strangled him," the hero said.

                                  Alcestis
Urged him again, "Stop here in Thessaly
As you come home."

                        "Perhaps you'd like a colt
Out of those mares for the young prince to break."

  "If you promise that the colt won't eat my children."

  "If it takes a nip, I'll eat the mares myself."

  He made his exit, and the quiet court
Resumed its known dimensions. Wall and column
Crept back into perspective, and the sun
Was present again, a little farther westward.
"Hell has been harrowed in our tranquil house,"
The king said wearily. "Are we all safe?"

  "I fear that Hercules has been offended,"
Eugenius reproached him.

                        "Why think that?
You heard him speak of coming back again.
He left in high good humor. He's a child.

He has the innocence of nature itself.
Simplicity like his won't take offense
At metaphysical questions. If it does,
The storm blows over quickly."

                              "Nonetheless,
You played a dangerous game with him, Admetus."
   "That I admit, and I have learned my lesson.
You know, temptation had me by the throat
To see what sort of notion a god might form,
A demigod at least, on the crucial point,
The point of his divine paternity.
I couldn't lose the chance."

                         "At such a time,"
Eugenius said, "when help in any form,
Divine help, could we gain it—"

                              "If you please,"
The king begged, "none of that. Men turn to the gods
In sickness. I will turn to them in health
Or not at all. Besides, my object was
To lead the conversation, if I could,
To some point that might help us. I lost out.
It wouldn't have done to push it any further.
But that was my real purpose."

                                Bion appeared
And signaled for attention at the door.
    "What is it, Bion?"

                        "Apollodorus, the priest,
Wishes to speak with you."

                            "It's as I feared.
They've got the start, Eugenius. Evil is first;
Unready reason toils to overtake it.
Is it an oracle? Have they an oracle, Bion?"

    "I am allowed to be the messenger
But not to speculate about the business,"
Bion said sleekly.

                    "Tell him to come in."
    Admetus waved dismissal, and the priest
Replaced the figure of Bion at the door.
    "Well?" said the king.

                        "Apollo has vouchsafed
An oracle."

                The king said to Alcestis,
"Vouchsafe his pompous tongue! It's not enough
To spread corruption in my people's minds.
He must corrupt our good Thessalian speech
With his cant terms. Well, out with it, let's hear it,"

                        · 32 ·

He told the priest.

                  "In this whole company?"

  "An oracle is fit for all to hear

Or fit for none."

              "The sentence of Apollo

Lies heavy on this court."

                    "Put the man off,"

Eugenius said in a whisper of alarm.

"Hear him in private. You are near exhaustion,

And what's to come—"

                  "Let it be now," the king said.

"I have borrowed strength from Hercules. Tomorrow

The fever may be worse, I may be dead.

We'll have the mischief over with. Come, man,

Out with it, speak your piece, and speak it plainly,

No canting and vouchsafing."

                    "The king's illness

Is fatal," said the priest.

              Alcestis leaned

And touched her husband's face. Admetus paled.

"This is a safe word for a god to say,"

He answered, smiling thinly. "Health itself

Is a disease that's fatal in the end.

Have you finished? Is this all?"

"The gods allow
One way by which Admetus may be saved."

"I knew, I knew there would be!" cried Alcestis.

"Don't trust it," said the king. "The rotten nut
Will show the nest of worms it has inside.
He hasn't cracked it yet."

"If any man
Or any woman offers in free will
To die in the king's place, the king shall live,
And on the man who offers his own life
The sentence of the gods will fall instead."

The king's wrath burst. "I said, Eugenius,
Always a priest will have his victim. Blood,
The purge of ignorance! You man of evil,
You think we'll whip some superstitious peasant
Or starve some petty thief until his life
Hangs rotten on his bones like leprosy
And makes him whimper for your knives to end it!"

"We need no knives. The god's word in itself
Will execute itself."

"You have done your part.
Leave us," the king said. "You disgust my manhood."

The priest withdrew.

                    "This is their pretty scheme,
This is the rotten fruit of their connivance!
What do you think of priests and priestcraft now?"

    "Say what you will, the oracle is known,
Or will be, to the last peasant in the kingdom,"
Eugenius answered. "It must be acted on.
I am sure your people will not be remiss."

    "I see. You think some fool will offer himself.
Then I shall have an enviable role!
I must thank him for my life, and he must die."

    "What else?" Eugenius asked.

                         "I am bewildered!
I search your faces," cried the king, "and all
Are vacant with submission. Will none of you
Look sane enough to blow this oracle
Into contempt? Come then, I'll try you all.
Eugenius, will you be the victim? You,
Life-servant of my kingdom? You, I fear,
Believe this oracle."

                    "If you do not,
You speak in irony," Eugenius answered.
"Allow me to reply in the same vein.

I'll let some man of less charge in the state
Come forward first."

                         "Where shall I look for help?
Mother, do you believe this oracle?"

   "Son, I have brought you up to fear the gods.
These tidings are a dreadful shock to us.
Your father will not sleep a wink all night.
But you have been a kind king to your people
And one of them will gladly die for you."

   "Do what you told the priest," said the king's father.
"Take that Levantine fellow, that Phoenician,
Doctor, he calls himself, but he's a spy.
He teaches slaves to read. His skin is greasy.
Flog him until he doesn't want to live.
Put him in irons in a dirty cell
And starve him till he catches some disease."

   "How can you think such cruelty," said Alcestis,
"Even to save your son? I offer myself—"

   "Stop!" cried Eugenius and caught her arm
In a rough grip of fear. "Don't speak, Alcestis!
You don't know what you say."

                        She drew herself
Gently out of his grasp and spoke again.

"I offer myself to bear my husband's fate."

She smiled, as if the issue were quite clear,
But the king cried, "The oracle is a lie!
You cannot mean, it is impossible
That you believe it."

      "What is this belief
You men, with all your metaphysical questions,
Quarrel about so much? I cannot argue
Your metaphysics with you. I am a woman
And do as I am moved to do," she said.

 "But you have heard these others speak, Alcestis.
They all believe, and fear. At least they fear.
Have you no fear?"

      "Oh, I am often frightened,
But if I lived in terror for myself
I could not live at all."

      "Ah," said the king,
"One honest and brave answer. Now, Alcestis,
We'll live in spite of them. We'll give the lie
To the priests and their mendacity."

        Alcestis
Leaned suddenly on Eugenius. In low voice,
Feeling the tremor of her arm, he said,

"What is it, Queen Alcestis? What's the matter?"
    "It's gone, I think. I felt the queerest pang.
It was quite dreadful."
                    "I wish you had not spoken."
    Admetus raised himself, straightened his back,
And looked from one to another. "Do you know,
I almost think I have passed the turn," he said.
"The fever has gone. My face and hands are cool."
    Eugenius felt the pressure on his arm
Increase until his age could scarcely bear
The weight of the queen's youth. "I am glad," she said.
"The children, they will have their father now."
    Amazed, as if the settled order of nature
Had cracked in boorish insult and spewed out
A grinning prodigy, the king leaped up
And sprang incredulous toward the fainting queen.

II

In one of the small rooms Admetus kept
For private entertainment stood a table
Covered with regally embroidered cloth,
And on the cloth stood plates and trenchers piled
With the havoc of choice roasts and loaves of bread
And a cone of fruit that like a shorn volcano
Had spilled its summit down its ragged slopes.
Before this devastation Hercules
The demigod stood holding at arm's length

A noble flagon, poised as if to pour
Into a golden goblet on the table,
The ripple of the slanted wine within
Darkly reflecting the pale tongues of light
From lamps along the walls. His other hand
Contained a delicate plum; his fingertips
Caressed it as a bear with calloused pads
Might fondle a puppy. He brought up the plum
In a loose arc under Eugenius' nose,
Who stood before him, watching hopefully
This last of many morsels first advance,
Then draw back from its natural destination.
    "Once and for all, friend," said the hero gruffly,
"The food and drink are all a man could ask.
Admetus can put on as good a table
As any king in Greece. Down in Mycenae
The food they give me isn't fit for swine.
Eurystheus, he won't throw a joint away
Until it's picked as clean as if the rats
Were in the pantry. Generally they are.
Did I say joint? Beans, beans is all I get.
Mud with some rabbit turds thrown in for flavor.
I'll tell you what I have to do down there:

I rustle cattle on the side for meat."

His eye enclosed Eugenius in a wink
Wide as a stable door. He belched, said "Pardon,"
And ate the plum.

               "I am glad," Eugenius told him,
"Our food and wine have proved acceptable."

   "Don't talk to me like an ambassador.
Acceptable!" He poured wine from the flagon
Into the goblet and above the rim.
The cloth of royal purple sponged it up,
And the dark stain spread from the golden base
In a creeping circle. "You aren't afraid of me?
I've noticed, times when people are afraid,
They use long words. That's one thing that I like
About Admetus, he isn't afraid of me.
The thing that scares me is a lot of talk
That I don't understand."

                    "I am afraid,
To tell the truth," Eugenius said and bowed.
"But only of this, that the king's ministers,
In the necessary absence of the king,
May fail to make his hospitality
As pleasant as the king would do himself."

"Well, well, another mouthful of hard words.
His necessary absence, is that it?
Where is he, then? You told me he was here.
Where is Admetus?"

                  "I've made my best endeavors,"
Eugenius said wearily, "to explain.
I've presented his apologies—"

                    "Endeavors!
Apologies! Mr. Ambassador,
You take the prettiest apology
You ever kissed or tickled on the rump
And what's her company good for? Where's Admetus?
You say he's well again?"

                  "Perfectly well,
If you mean by that recovered from his illness.
Would you like another shoulder of roast mutton?
Some of the goats' cheese we allow ourselves
To boast of here in Thessaly?"

                    "Just wine
To wash down what I've fed myself already."
  The hero proffered the goblet, but Eugenius
Bowed and declined. Hercules drank it off
And shook the flagon, testing it for more.

"Now here's a wine, on a winter night like this,
Warms a man's liver. Admetus is no king
To water his wine down as Eurystheus does.
A man comes in from the cold, frost on the ground,
Maybe he's covered fifty, sixty miles,
Walking from sunup, and a little wine
Does him no harm. I don't mean watered, either."

"You have there our best vintage, Hercules."

"Vintage! I've been drinking vintage, have I?
Well, wine or vintage, what it does, I say,
Is all that counts."

                "We hope this wine of ours
Has both authority and suavity."

"Suavity, is it! Well now, there's two drinks
I've had tonight I never had before,
Vintage and suavity. Come up here, vintage!
Come up here, suavity! Better drink fast
Before I'm scared to drink at all."

                      He drank

And smacked his lips.

                "Admetus is all right,
He got his health back, did he? That's good news.
I've never had a sick day in my life,

Unless it was the times I lost my head
And did things that I never meant to do.
That was a kind of sickness, you might say."

"Perhaps I can explain in similar terms
Just why Admetus cannot see you now,"
Eugenius said hopefully. "The king
Is well in body, but a sore affliction
Troubles his mind."

                    "What, out of his wits?
Why didn't you tell me? Has he killed somebody?"

"No, no, not mad, nor guilty of a crime.
No death here at the court lies on his hands.
The gods appoint our times to live and die.
The mind has other afflictions, Hercules,
Than crime or madness. How can I explain
Except as I have tried to do already?"

"You talk in riddles, that's what I don't like.
I've never met the job I couldn't do,
But if I had to guess the Sphinx's riddle,
I'll tell you what, I'd solve it right enough,
I'd choke the Sphinx, and then I'd throw her carcass
Over a cliff."

                    Hercules drank again

And glared around as if to find a victim
On whom he might exhibit then and there
The art of cutting short a tangled question.
  "I'm sorry if I've spoken mysteries.
I did not mean to," said Eugenius.
"You know how keen a conscience the king has
Toward hospitality. He always calls it
The first of obligations."
                  "Obligations!
I'm just an obligation, is that it?
Mr. Apology sends his kind regards
To Mr. Obligation, and good-by!
I see it now. Admetus gives me food
And wine to wash it down with—is that right?"
  "His pleasure is to offer you his best."
  "And sends apologies and gibblegabble
Instead of his own company—that right?"
  "He does not want to thrust a private grief
On you, his guest, his great and valued friend."
  "I've worn my welcome out in Thessaly,
That's what it all comes down to. It's the same
As in Mycenae. Any jobs to do,
I'm demigod, I'm hero, Hercules.

But am I wanted in the house? Oh no!
Come within spitting distance of the palace,
I'm Mr. Obligation, just a big mouth.
Give him some food and drink and let him go!"
    The hero's face became a parody
Of childlike hurt and shame and helpless rage.
"I'll tell you what Admetus wants!" he roared.
"He wants to see my ass go down the road
And never hear a fart from me again!"
    Eugenius lifted supplicating hands.
    "I beg you, Hercules, if ever you cared
For Admetus and his court, or for his queen,
Do not desert them now. Do not depart
In anger or resentment. Put on me
All blame for the miscarriage of my mission.
Apollo would redouble the king's despair
If you imagined that his welcoming hand
Is not sincere because he cannot come
To offer it himself. Wait for an hour,
Two hours at most. The time will be too short
Till all is clear."
                    The hero stood in doubt,
Then partly mollified he said, "Well, friend,

You sound as though you meant it. I can wait.
I'll take you at your word."

                    He raised the goblet.
"How is the queen?" he asked. "How is Alcestis?"
  Eugenius winced before the dreaded question.
"She is—not herself," he said with difficulty.

  "What's that? She isn't herself? Who is she, then?
Has she been turned into a basilisk
By one of these meta— what's the word I mean?"

  "A metamorphosis? No, Hercules,
The queen is not in health."

                    "Why didn't you say so?
The trouble with you is too much education.
You can't talk in plain words. It couldn't be
Another little prince is on the way,
Or a little princess? Let me be the midwife!
I'll hold him up and give his rump a spank,
I'll make a king of him with his first squawk!"

  "The queen is not in childbed," said Eugenius.

  "Is she very sick? Are you afraid she'll die?
Don't be afraid of that. Alcestis die?
I'll carry her in my arms all over Greece,
I'll beard the immortal gods on Mount Olympus—

Where is she now?"

                The hero's eagerness
Beetled over Eugenius, drove him back
A pace or two, and with constricted voice
He said, "She is past danger."

                       "If that's so,
She's getting better, she'll be well again."
  Eugenius bowed.

                "You say she is past danger?"
  "Yes," said the old man wearily.

                    "I'm glad,
Glad to hear that," said Hercules. "It's plain
I came at a bad time. I'd best be off."
  "Let me implore you, Hercules, not to leave us.
Admetus charged me as a solemn duty
To make you feel at home."

               "Well, then, I'll stay.
I'll do just as he wants."

               The old man sighed,
A long sigh of relief. "If you'll forgive me,
I'll say good night, and send the poet Bion
To entertain you and see that you receive
Whatever you need until you want to sleep."

"Bion, you say? A poet? He doesn't sound
Like much for company, but trot him in,
I'll look his paces over. Maybe he knows
A song or two."

                  Eugenius bowed his leave,
And Hercules drank, humming a wordless bar.
Bion came in, his lyre beneath his arm,
And Hercules eyed him. "You must be the poet
That what's-his-name, the old ambassador,
Told me about. Well, wet your whistle, boy,
And settle down, we'll make a night of it."

  He thrust the goblet into Bion's hand
And pushed him toward a divan. Bion drank,
Cautiously, with an estimating eye
On the condition of his giant host.

  "May I ask, Hercules, of your success
In your latest labor? I could turn the story
Into an ode, or work it into an epic
Combining all your labors."

                   "Oh, those mares?
They're all outside here in the stable now,
Gentle as mice. Man-eating mares, they said,
But they all followed me along like colts

Trotting across the pasture by their dams.
It was a little rough on Diomedes,
But that was strictly in the way of business."

"What was his fate, if you don't mind my asking?"

"You want to know? As I antipicated—
Is that the word I mean?"

                              "Anticipated?"

"As I expected, he didn't want to lose
Those mares of his. He doesn't have much to show
Around that little court he keeps in Thrace.
I don't know that I blame him. Anyway,
I had to break his neck. You understand,
I hadn't a thing against him. That's a point
You want to remember when you kill a man.
Just do it in the regular line of business,
Meaning no harm, and then it isn't a crime."

"If you could give me a few particulars,
What he said and what you said, a few details
To get me started—"

                        "Let the epic wait.
There's lots of time, boy. Never mind it now.
Let's both get mellow. What about a song?
Here, wet your whistle, no one can sing dry."

While Bion put the goblet to his lips,
Keeping a watchful eye across the brim,
Hercules cradled an imagined lyre
And delicately plucked it. "How's for this one?

When the Argonauts in days of old
Set sail in their leaky lugger,
They were a band of heroes bold
And every one was a
                    Kalalalalonioudleoipsioi!

Know it?" he asked.
                    "No, I'm afraid I don't.
But I could learn it. How does it go on?"
    "I can't remember. I don't recollect
My memory was ever good for much.
There's one thing comes to mind, though. Have I told you
About the first time that I killed a man?
Give me that lyre, I'll show you how it was."
    He seized the lyre from Bion, who leaned back,
Carefully indolent, braced on both his elbows,
And slowly slid his legs across the divan
To put them on the far side from his host.
    "I was no bigger than a half-grown pup,"
Said Hercules, his eye rapt by the scene

He meant to re-create. "I was learning music.
Now you're my teacher, see? Only in fact
He was a bald old scarecrow with a breath
Like rotten melon. I was holding the lyre,
And down he sticks his cheek right by my mouth
To show me something I did wrong. Remember,
I was a little brat, like this—"

                       He squatted,
Bringing the grizzled ringlets of his hair
Opposite Bion's chin. Bion let down
His legs across the divan, felt the floor,
And inched his body after them.

                       "Like this,"
The hero said. "He stuck his rotten breath
Into my face, and what did I do then,
Not thinking? That was when I first found out
How strong I was. I upped that lyre, I did,
And bashed his brains out."

                       Hercules towered up
Suddenly, with a flexure of his legs,
And swung the lyre in a tremendous blow
That hung arrested, sculptured in mid-air,
When he saw the divan vacant underneath him.

"Well, so you're gone, old hooknose. Just as well.
It's just as well for both of us, I guess.
I might have killed you again. What's happened here?
Have they left me all alone?"

                              He glared about,
But saw no sign of Bion in the room.
He tossed the lyre on the divan, raised the goblet
And found it empty, the flagon empty too.
"What about wine in here," he shouted. "Wine!"

   He took a moody stride or two. A boy,
Timid, and clutching a flagon in both hands,
Came in and set it shakily on the table.

   "Now there's a little soldier," said the hero.
"What's your name? You're as pretty as a girl."

   He put forth a great finger, chucked the boy
Under the chin, and pinched him on the buttocks.
The child screamed and ran crying from the room.

   "Now who's out of his head?" the hero roared.
"Me, or the whole court? What's the matter here?"

   The question battered the walls. Eugenius entered
And asked what might be wrong.

                              "You tell me, friend,"
Said Hercules. "You're at the bottom of this,

You and your mysteries and your gibblegabble.
I have a mind to take you by the neck
And teach you how to talk plain words. Now listen:
Where is Admetus? I want to see Admetus."

  "One moment, if you will," the old man sighed.

  Hercules menaced his retreating back
With a look such as a savage forest gives
To a traveler reaching the tilled fields at dusk.
He paced the little room and brought up short
At each close angle of the walls in turn.
He poured the goblet full, but as he raised it
The king, Admetus, entered. He put it down,
Untasted, and the king came forward quickly,
Haggard in face, though with full bodily vigor.

  "I had not meant," he said, "to thrust on you
The sorrows of my court. It would have been
The truer part of courtesy to spare you,
Or so I thought. Forgive me, Hercules,
And—pity me."

                    "Pity?" said Hercules.
"Tell me what's happened. What is it all about?
Take 'em coming and going, man and boy,
I've drunk ten people under the table there

· 54 ·

And not a one to tell me in plain words—"
  "Did Eugenius tell you nothing?"
                        "Which was he?
I know the one, the old ambassador,
Talked a lot of mystifigation at me.
All I made out, he said the queen was sick
But now she's out of danger."
                    "Those were the words,
The words I put into his mouth myself.
'We think she is past danger.' How could I cavil
And play upon her life as on a phrase,
Yet how could I have found a truer word?"
  "My head is going to split right down the seams!
How is Alcestis? How is she? Tell me that!"
  "If you had heard the oracle, Hercules!
No word of it has reached you?"
                        "Oracle?
What oracle? I've gone from here to Thrace,
I've done some walking since I saw you last,
Haven't been off my legs except for sleep
Since autumn ended. I've brought those mares along.
They're tied up in your stables now, Admetus.
I was going to give the queen a little colt—

Carried it all the way from Thrace, I did,
Holding it in my arms."

                     "The oracle,
The sentence of Apollo on my court!
I never believed it, and I do not now
Believe it, and I never shall believe it.
Yet the coincidence—"

                     "Coincidence?
Give me a plain word, tell me how the queen is,
Or I'll go mad and break somebody's neck."

  "Be patient with me. You shall hear it all
To the last deadly clarity of truth.
The oracle—we must begin with that.
'The king's disease is fatal'—so the words went—
'But if any man or woman freely offers
To die instead, Admetus shall recover
And death shall fall upon his substitute.'
Alcestis, yes, Alcestis, who but she
Spoke, and offered to die for me, her husband!
Oh, past all reason, not to be believed,
The malice of coincidence at work
Like two accomplice thieves with superstition,
Yet from the very moment that she spoke

I had my health and she had my disease
Or one so like it that I must have breathed
My own corruption down her willing throat
With a kiss that will forever haunt my bed.
O my poor girl, my queen, my faithful saint!
If you could see her, Hercules, her life,
Her youth, her quickness burned with a damp flame
So that her hair is clammy with the sweat
And yet no sip drawn from the coldest spring
Can cool her thirsty lips or comfort them!"
   "But now she's out of danger, that's what he said,
That's what you both said."
                    "Oh yes, past all danger,
For while we live we are in daily danger,
But when we die then we have left behind
All dangers and all trials that life sets us."
   The voice of Hercules rose to a blast.
"But is she dead or is she still alive?"
   "I have sat beside her bed," Admetus answered,
"And seen and heard the last breath come and go
A hundred times, I thought."
                 "Then she's alive!
Quick, to her room. I'll catch him as he comes,

I'll beat him from the door, I'll rattle the dice
He carries in his moldy chaps!"

                    The king
Smiled wearily. "What, conquer death by force?
I know you would do it for me if you could.
But I have reached the point that many men
Have reached before, the point at which we say,
'It is better that she should not suffer longer.'
Slip away now, poor girl, and have your rest,
You have so nearly finished the long journey."

   Hercules caught Admetus by the neck
And raised him to his toes. "Where is her room?
I know the slave, I tell you. Touch Alcestis?
I'll tear him from her throat. I'll snap his bones
Like a rotten weedstalk. Take me where she is!"

   He hustled Admetus toward the door. The king,
Weeping with sorrow and humiliation,
Had no choice but to lead him toward the room
Where even then a woman held a mirror
To the queen's lips, and found it still discolored
By the moist breath that showed she was alive.

III

In a stony valley, among sand and thorns,
A landscape visible only here and there
In wandering lichen-patches of gray light,
Yet certainly stone, certainly thorns and sand,
A woman moved, hooded and robed in folds
Of a dull sheen, a woman certainly,
Though, like the stones and thorns and the gray sand,

Never complete in form, but showing now
No more than a vague turn of shrouded arm,
Yet certainly an arm, and now her head
Bowed under pressure of a driving weight.

    She moved in faltering steps, two steps or three,
And then resisted, standing and faintly swaying,
As if her feet were roots in the gray sand,
As if they were the pedestal of a statue
From which her body struggled to escape.
Slowly her head lifted the heavy weight
That drove her, and her arms rose heavily
And her hands clasped in a gesture of entreaty.
Slowly she turned and strained against her feet,
Slowly revolved, as if to struggle back
Along the uncertain way that she had come.
But it was not allowed her to return.
Again with bowed head driven along her path
She moved irregularly, propelled by force
Though following no direction. From the stones
And from the dusk above the thorns and sand
A voice came, uttering a troubled question,
The voice of Queen Alcestis.

                        "Where am I?"

Alcestis asked, and the robed figure, pausing,
Lifted her hands and groped as if to touch
Door posts or walls that some malignant will
Had stolen away.

             "Alone," Alcestis said,
"I am alone."

          The woman covered her face,
Bowed and immovable.

               "Where is alone?
Oh, that's profound, that question is profound!"
  So said the queen, and laughed a few low notes
As if a thrush were there beside a brook,
As if the shadows over the dry sand,
Hiding Alcestis, could hide water too,
The music of a brook over bright stones.
Then the queen sighed, and from the shadows where
Her life was no more than a speaking nerve
Amid the thorns and sand, her voice went on.
  "We have a place," she said, "when we are with
The people whom we love, who look to us
And we to them. We know just where we are,
Even if they have gone to the next room
Or on a journey. But now I am alone.

I don't know where I am or where I'm going."
    With heavy steps the figure in the sand
Circled a weary measure or two and stopped,
Lifted her head, and with a questioning air
Looked one way and another. Then her pace
Became a frenzy of impeded struggle,
As if she tore herself against the force
That drove her by the neck and bound her feet
In heavy sand. Alcestis cried, her voice
Forcing its way by will through her clenched throat,
"Admetus! Where have you gone? Admetus, tell me!
Where am I? Why have you left me all alone?"
    The shrouded figure stood amid the sand,
Imploring, and where pity would not come,
Pitied herself with her beseeching arms.
    "At times he is close beside me," said the queen,
"And then he is far off. Why, just this moment
I saw him plainly, walking on ahead,
Hardly a step ahead. Admetus, wait!
I cannot go so fast. Show me the way.
Why do you hurry? Now he's gone again.
Sometimes he turns and laughs, and then he runs
And hides himself behind these little hills,

And when I reach the place an ugly mountain
Towers and shakes above my head, and rocks
Fly out and fall like gray birds in the air."
   The woman in the sand cowered and shrank,
And waited for the tumbling of the rocks
To rain and patter on her back.
                          "Just now
He was right behind me. I was going to touch him,"
The queen said, "I was going to clasp his hand.
'I will be faithful,' that's what I meant to say.
'I'll keep my promise, really I will, Admetus.
I'll go, I'll make the journey to the end.'
But when I put my hand out, it was dust.
A stream of dust, like tickling grains of meal,
Ran from my arm."
                   The cowering figure straightened,
Put forth a long robed arm that ran with dust
In a never-emptying stream, a chute of dust
Like meal poured from a bin.
                     "He gave me a push,"
Alcestis said, "he gave me a hard push."
   The shrouded figure lurched and stumbled forward
And nearly fell.

"And then I felt him run.
He ran until he flew, flew far behind me,
Flew like an ember on the winter wind
And blinked out like the small eye of a spark.
I have not seen him since."

                The hue of light
Over the sand, over the stones and thorns,
Brightened an instant like a splitting coal.
The robed head and the bowed and driven back
Leaped into form against the uncertain flare
And then were dim again.

                "Oh, there I am!"
Alcestis said. "Now I can see myself.
I understand. I often dream this way.
One part of me is there, and I can watch it
Almost as if it were another person,
Yet really all the time I'm right here, too.
And I know what will happen next. Both parts,
The over-there part and the right-here part,
Will come together suddenly. That means
Another person, really another person,
Is coming into the dream. It's very queer.
I'm going to be afraid, I know I am.

But if I need to, I can wake myself.
This is the way I do, crouch down like this,
And look all round, look carefully all round,
And then I jump, I jump up and I scream!"
  Slowly the robed and hooded woman crouched
And wriggled slyly on the stones and sand,
And laid her cheek on this side and on that,
Looking with pale eyes upward and about.
She writhed and tried to spring, and her mouth opened
But could not scream, nor could her knees release
The tension of their huddled agony.
She rose as if her will were steeped and thickened
In a slow drug and stood uncertainly,
And then with a wavering and a floating motion
She glided toward Alcestis, merged with her
In the shadows where the queen stood; and the queen
Came forward bowed and slow across the sand,
Plodding and circling in the same weary measure,
Impelled by the same force on the same path
That followed no direction.
                              "I am driven,
Driven along," Alcestis said. "My promise
Drives me along. I go because I promised.

Where am I going? When will the journey end?"

　　She stopped and turned as far as she could turn,
From head to breast, from breast to thigh, from thigh
Down to the knee and ankle, then no more.
Slowly the painful revolution ceased,
Reversed itself, and she went slowly on,
Circling and plodding in the heavy sand.

　　"I am not alone. Now I am not alone.
Someone is at my back," she said. "I feel him
Although I cannot see him. He is the one
Who forces me along this dreary path.
He made the tickling dust run from my arm.
He will not let me turn, but I will turn!"

　　Her hands made ropes out of the empty shadow,
And clawing them, she tore and twisted round
And lurched and shuffled back along her path
Until she stood with lifted head and breast
Confronting the tall robes and golden mask
That stalked her wandering progress

　　　　　　　　　　　　"Ah," she said,
"I thought some horrible thing—"

　　　　　　　　　　　　Her breath drained out
In a long sighing whisper of relief.

· 66 ·

He stood enclosed and self-revealed in light,
With folded arms, and blind majestic head
Masked in the sculptured likeness of a god,
With golden ringlets brightly crowned and bearded
And golden cheeks and calm full lips of gold.

    "I think I know you, do I not? Just now
I am so confused," she said. "You must forgive me.
I can't recall your name."

                    The golden eyes
And the bright ringlets of the golden mask,
The cheeks, the lips, replied but made no motion,
Only inclining gravely toward the queen
And courteously speaking.

                  "Who I am
You know, Alcestis, and you do not know.
You are not yet ready to be told my name.
It will come to you of itself when you are ready."

    "At least I am not alone. I'm glad of that.
I'd rather go with almost anyone
Than all alone." She laughed. "How thoughtless of me!
I should explain that I am on a journey."

    "And I have come to be your guide, Alcestis."

    "If I were sure of that! Who are you, then?"

The folds beneath the glitter of the mask
Moved a tall pace or two, and the queen followed.
   "I am called a god, Alcestis."

                        The queen laughed
As a girl laughs at flattery too open.
   "Am I walking with a god, then? That for me
Is much too great an honor. But so I felt
When I became a king's wife and a queen."
   "I also am a husband and a king."
   "Enough for me that I am Queen Alcestis,
Wife to Admetus, King of Thessaly."
   "Is it enough, Alcestis? Where is he now,
Your king, your royal husband?"

                       "Oh, as for that,
He is not far away, although just where—
Do you know? Can you tell me? Oh, you have taken him,
You have turned him against me. But he will come back,
He'll understand. Admetus, help, I need you!"
   Alcestis reeled like a tormented flower,
Blown by a gust, but could not lift her feet
To run and flog the sand in frantic search.
The sightless golden mask above the robes
Waited and stood until the straining flower

Rose upright and was tremulously quiet.

"I am your husband now, I am your king.
You must come with me, Alcestis, to my kingdom.
You must be my queen. The journey has been hard.
It is almost over now. We are nearly there.
Only a little way, a little farther.
Come, Queen Alcestis."

                    "Only a little way?
I should be glad to reach the end and rest.
I am very tired."

                    "Yield then, Alcestis. Come."

    The queen sighed with the breath of summer wind
That gathers at the edge of a long grove
And sweeps it softly till the last thin leaf
Has whispered and grown silent. Timidly
She tried a voluntary pace or two
And found the progress easier, and walked
Lightly in circling measures through the sand,
Then stopped and stood again.

                            "I have my kingdom,"
She said defiantly. "I have my children.
I will not go with you."

                    "Ah yes, your children.

Will they remember you? How long, Alcestis?
You think they need you, and indeed they do,
But they will live and be the stronger for it
Without your tenderness."

       "I have not spoiled them.
I have brought them up like princes and like queens.
Ah, you should see them, learning to play the harp,
Learning to ride, or going about their games!
You should see my little Eumelus break the colt
His father gave him! Children, where have you gone?
Come, it is time for lessons."

       "They do not come.
They cannot help you now, nor you help them,
Weary Alcestis. Yield, follow your guide.
You have no duty now except to rest,
And all rest lies in yielding. Come, my queen!"

  Alcestis moved, her knees lightened again,
Her feet found liberty amid the sand.
A little way she moved, circling and walking,
And the golden eyes followed with selfless calm.

  Again she stopped and stood. "Where is your kingdom?
What people do you rule? Will they receive me
As if I were a queen, or as a stranger,

In hatred and contempt?"

                 "My kingdom lies
In the shadow of oblivion, sweeter far
Than all the shade of oak trees, or of glens
Where the snake crawls beneath the rhododendrons
And the lynx gorges on the spotted fawn
Whose doe has gone to drink. None there is thirsty,
No man is killed in war, none hurt in hunting.
No woman whimpers by the winter coals,
Alone and toothless, chewing on the cud
That memory brings into her wandering thought
Like bitter sorrel."

               "Are there no flowers there,
No smell of hyacinth, no breeze at evening
Blowing across the mountains or the sea?
Are there no children laughing, or quarreling
So that a word can make them happy again?
Eumelus! Look, do you see him there? Eumelus,
Bring me a cup of water, there's a good boy!
Oh, I could be refreshed by one cool sip
Of the water from our clear Thessalian spring!"

  "My kingdom is your water and your bread,
Your coolness and refreshment. Come, and drink."

"Take me there. I am ready," said the queen,
And moved a step or two, and then stood frightened
And cried out, "No, not yet. You must not touch me.
Don't touch me. Help, Admetus! What shall I do?
How can I go with him and yet be faithful?
Where shall I turn for help?"

      "To me, Alcestis.
Bride of my kingdom, queen among my queens,
Come, yield!"

    Slowly and slyly Alcestis
Lowered her head and turned her face away
And her eyes glittered with a sidelong cunning.
And then, as if she had won a struggle of wits,
She cried out, "So! You have a queen already!
Out of your lips I heard it! Many queens,
Captives and concubines! Would you make me,
Wife to Admetus, a royal slave and whore
At whom men spit and suck their lips with envy?"

 She flogged and floundered over the gray sand
In a slow frenzy of escape. Her feet
Labored and struggled; her knees flexed wide and gaped
As if to gulp up space in frantic flight,
But all her violence carried only a step,

Two steps or three, across the heavy sand.
Panting and cowering, she stood and searched.
Her arms implored the shadows, and her face
Implored; and in the uncertain dusk and distance
Among the sad harsh stones and thorny hillocks
The semblance of a light appeared and grew,
And in the light, a girl seated and crowned
On a dull throne, and lovely in dejection.
In her lap, beneath the hollow of her breast,
She held a withered sheaf of flowers. Alone
She sat, and she was speaking to herself,
Or singing, for the clear unhappy voice
Was like a song in hell.

                    "Oh, that my mother,"
So the girl sang, "would send a dove or swallow
Down to my prison, that it might bring me here
In my long exile but one sprig of green,
One stolen violet from the mountain vales,
Or cup of laurel brimming with fresh rain!
This withered sheaf I carry for remembrance
Preserves no more even the form of flowers.
Oh, I should welcome and warm you, visiting swallow!
See, I should hold you here between my breasts

And give you the soft comfort of my hands!

    "But no, the swallows on their roving wings
Have all gone forth, and far from wintry Greece
Found summer for themselves in other lands.
The mountain vales are white with snow, and I,
Locked in my dreary prison half the year,
The childless wife of a cold barren king,
Must bide and wait, must wait, until at last
My prison opens, and I return to earth.
Then shall I breathe the warm quick air again
And all the flowers follow at my heels
As I walk on the bright lawns with my mother."

    The voice ceased, and the crowned girl on her throne
Was gone; but in a craze of dread and triumph
Alcestis cried, "There, there! Did you see there?
I know that lady! The girl Persephone
Whom you unkindly ravished from her mother
And hold in your dark prison half the year!"

    The golden robes and the tall mask moved forward
And menaced her.

              "Liar and ravisher,
You have deceived me! I know you, who you are,"
The queen shrieked, and she thrust with hands and nails

Into the godlike mask, scratched, clawed, and raked
With rigid nails and fingers, and the mask
Melted like slime in which the heads of snakes
Lie with unblinking eyes above their coils.
The dazzling brightness turned to a thick slime
And the skewed features crawled and dripped like slime,
And underneath was death. The robes and skull
Fell on the queen and forced her knees apart
And threw her to the ground, and from her mouth,
Instead of the long scream for which it opened,
Issued an animal groan. Then through the valley,
Among the stones and in the wavering dusk,
Came sounds of an impatient tread of feet
Beating and harrying back and forth with steps
That rattled the dry thorns, and a voice roared,
Threshing the shadows with its rough approach,
"Alcestis! Lady! Queen! Is the slave there?
Is the dog at you? Show me where he is!"
    The robes and skull rose from between her knees
And stood with watchful dignity. The feet
Pounded like mallets on the sand; the voice
Drew closer.
            "Tell me where he is, Alcestis.

Give me a sight of him, I'll make him skip.
I see you now. Out of the way, old bones!
Touch her, and if I leave a piece of you
Big as a knuckle, don't call me Hercules!"
    "The queen is mine," the skull said, drawing back
Before the hero's bearded fists. "If now
You cheat me of her with your vulgar strength,
Still she is mine. I'll have her in the end."
    "We'll see to that when the time comes," said the hero.
    The tall robes leaned and ducked this way and that
As if to circumvent and slip behind
Their rude antagonist, then turned and shrank
With a defeated leer, and slow at first,
Then swiftly, gathered pace across the sand
And vanished in the distance.
                                          "He is gone,"
Alcestis said. "Do you think he's really gone?
He flew off just the way Admetus flew.
He did, you know. He ran and flew far off
And left me all alone."
                                          "He won't come back,
You needn't be afraid of that, Alcestis.
I told Admetus what I'd do to him.

I said I'd wring him out like an old kilt
If he so much as touched a hair of yours.
How are you, lady? Here, let me help you up."
    He bent and raised her with rough gentleness.
    "I am better," said the queen. "A moment past
It seemed as though a fresh wind cooled my face.
It seemed as though I drank a sip of water.
Don't take your hand away. It gives me strength."
    Hercules held the queen's hand awkwardly
As if it were a white, exhausted bird.
    "I know just how you feel. You're tired and hot.
And times like that," he said, "there's nothing better
Than a smart breeze. I know, I've tramped the hills
Along the Aegean, sweaty and tired of walking,
And watched the fishing boats heel over sharp
When catspaws hit them, and felt the wind come fresh,
Or sometimes when I've been in Thessaly
I've come to one of those cold mountain springs
You have there, and I've got down on my knees
And soused my head all over."
                                        He restored
The queen's hand. With a smile she walked away
And smoothed her hair.

"It seems almost as though
I had drunk from such a spring myself," she said.

"The fever's going down, that's what it means.
You'll be back again with Admetus and the children
Before a man can say 'Jove's mistresses'."

"The children! Oh, I'll want them, I know I shall,
After a time. But now I'm still so tired,
I want to be myself a little while."

"Well, naturally, you need a lot of rest."

Alcestis smiled, and turned again, and walked
Somewhat away, looking for him to follow,
Then smoothed herself about her waist and knees,
And turning back she stood beneath his face,
Seeking his eye.

                    "You saved me, Hercules."

"Oh," said the hero, "you'd have beaten him off
If I'd been herding geese down in Mycenae."

"You are stronger than death himself."

                              "Well, that's as may be.
I guess I'm strong enough for a day's work.
It's all I'm fit for. What's that word he called me?
Vulgar? I'll have that out with him someday.
I won't let anyone call me my right name

If I don't like it."

    "You have conquered death.
You tore me from his hands, you brought me back
From the borders of his kingdom," said Alcestis,
And strained on tiptoe, lifting up her hands
To put them on his shoulders.

      "Now, Alcestis,
I ought to take you back," said Hercules,
"Back to Admetus and the little ones."

 "But did Admetus help me," asked the queen,
"When I needed him and called him? He ran off,
He left me. It was you who brought me help.
You rescued me from death, not he."

       "Now, now,
Admetus never left you, don't say that.
It was the oracle, it all began—"

 "Hercules, don't you even want to kiss me?"

 "I know what makes you talk this way. It's fever.
The fever hasn't gone yet," said the hero.
"It's queer what notions people get with fever.
It's like a madness, it makes you want to do
Things you would never do in your right mind."

 "I really think one story is a lie

· 79 ·

That people tell about you, Hercules."

"A pack of them are lies."

"One is, I'm sure,
That one about King Thespius and his daughters."
Alcestis laughed. "Admetus would be shocked
If he knew that I had even heard that story."

Hercules mopped his forehead. "Now, Alcestis,
What made you think of that? It isn't right
To bring that up. You shouldn't think of it!"

"Thespius the king had fifty daughters,"
Chanted Alcestis, laughing. "Thespius
Dispatched them one by one for fifty nights
To Hercules, and each proud girl came back
A maid no longer, and each bore a son.
It's false, it's false!"

She danced upon her toes
And wrung her hands with laughter.

Hercules
Raised a great helpless palm and squeezed the air.
"You shouldn't bring that up against me now,
But as for truth—"

"It's true then, Hercules?"
"Don't hold me for details, I can't remember.

But all these stories start—"

                          "Ah," said Alcestis,

Dejected and appealing, "I see now!

You could love all those fifty little sluts

And yet you can't love me. Oh, what a fright

This fever must have left me!"

                              "That's not so,

That's not the truth, Alcestis! They were sluts,

That's right enough, those girls old Thespius had.

But you, Alcestis, you are beautiful,

A queen, a lady. Oh, I had a wife,

My Deianeira, she was a pretty thing,

As beautiful as you, with little ways

And a soft voice like yours, and then I killed her.

The madness came, I choked her with my hands

And tore and strangled, tore my children too.

Oh, not for me, not for my hands to tear

And make the blood and flesh run on the floor,

Beauty and kindness and a woman's ways

Like yours, Alcestis, no, no, not for me,

Never in all the world from here to Egypt!

I'm a rough man, fit only for rough work."

  "Poor Hercules!"

"Come along now, Alcestis.
I'll take you to Admetus and the children."
   "If you think he wants me, I will come," she said.
   "That's better! Now you talk like Queen Alcestis.
You come, I'll help you find the way."
                              She sighed,
And turned as though unready, turned and walked
A circling measure through the sand and shadows.
The voice of Hercules grew faint, his tread
Diminished in the dusk.
                    "I'll tell Admetus.
I'll let him know you're coming soon, Alcestis."
   The queen stood passively and let him go.
She stood amid the gray sand, waiting, looking.
   "I am alone," she said. "I am alone."
   Then in the shadows over the gray sand
Appeared the woman in dull hood and robes,
Walking and pausing.
                    "I can see myself,"
Said the queen's voice. "I can see where I am.
There I am, over there."
                    The circling figure
Followed no path, but lightly moved and walked.

"Now I can walk," the queen said. "Now my feet
Can go wherever I want."
                              The woman walked
This way and that, and skipped a pace or two
As children skip, and trailed her arms in the air
As if the soft resistance of the shadows
Flattered her freedom with its liquid touch.
   "The stream of hot dust running from my arm
Has stopped," Alcestis said. "My hand is healed.
The fingers are all there, as true as life.
Oh, it is good to feel my hand again."
   The woman laid her hand against her cheek
And touched it with her lips.
                              "I can even run,"
Alcestis said. "I believe that I can run."
   Slyly the woman crouched on the gray sand,
And looked about, and sprang. Her feet ran freely,
Her knees lifted and leaped. This way and that
She ran as if for some imagined goal,
And reaching it, she wheeled in a wild canter
And ran again in a frenzy of free motion.
   "I can run," Alcestis cried. "See how I run!
I leap and turn and run wherever I want.

I'm running, running! See how I leap and run!
Oh, this is better than going back again!
I'll come, Admetus, presently I'll come,
But now I'm running. See how I can run!"

Then the gray valley and the leaping figure
Darkened and ebbed away; and those who watched
At the bedside of the queen looked at each other
And marveling said, "Her brow is cool. She sleeps."

IV

Like white wine in a blue cup, the spring sunlight
Stood in the sky above the open court
Where Queen Alcestis, holding in her lap
A length of woven stuff, and in one hand
A wooden hoop, sat quietly at work
Pulling white threads through the rich purple ground
And watching her design creep slowly forward.

"To think!" the king said, pacing back and forth.
"Mistrust, contempt, malignity, all these

I have had to bear from my own court, my friends,
And bear them quite alone. If any man
Felt in his heart a grain of sympathy,
If any put himself in my position,
None has been bold enough to say as much.
I have been an outcast and a man tabu!
All these long months I have struggled without hope.
I have seen no chink in their hostility,
No point where I could pry a lever in
And crack their front. But now at last our priests
Have overstepped themselves. For the first time
I see a chance to beat them. In the end
I'll win, Alcestis. Time has fought my battle,
Time, and their recklessness. My turn comes round
To strike, and I have struck where they will feel it.
I dealt them my first blow this very day."

   The king looked round, halting his restless march
About the tranquil court, but the queen's head
Was bent above her work.

                 "You do not care,"
The king said bitterly. "You'd let me be
A slave in my own kingdom, taking orders
From those impostors for the sake of peace."

"I never wanted you to be a slave,"
Alcestis answered, lifting up her eyes
And looking at him gravely.

                    "But I would be!"
The king protested. "For all that I have said,
You do not understand. You do not see
What manner of men they are and what would follow
Should I admit this miracle of theirs.
Listen, Alcestis! On that winter night
When suddenly the fever left your face,
When your brow cooled and you began to live,
That oracle they cunningly hatched out,
That sentence of Apollo, as they called it,
Stood ready to be stripped as a bare fraud,
Exposed for what it was. But their luck held,
For Hercules came blundering by, and roared,
In full drink, he would drive death from your door.
They did not miss that shout. They seized their cue,
They are quick at that, I grant, and now we learn
That the great gods who sentenced me to die
And then transferred the doom from me to you
Relented, and allowed their drunken hero
To flout their sacred oracle. For this

The blood of bullocks and of rams must flow!
Ewes, heifers, doves, all useful fowls and fruits
That men have tamed or bred, smoke on their altars.
Appointed sacrifices fall far short
Of what this drunken miracle demands.
There must be special offerings day and night
Until the temple and the very palace
Reek with a dry unwholesome cloud of death
While priests grow fat and tipsy. For the grape
Is not neglected in their ceremonies.
Oh no, the grape is present lavishly!
The gods require libations, and the priests
Must tipple with their masters. But excess
Brings its own cure at last. The old saw is true.
Some of the wiser heads about the court
Begin to see the effects of oracles,
And miracles, and priestly superstition.
The herdsman tires of driving bulls to slaughter;
The shepherd sees his best ewes put to knife
And wonders where his flock will be next year.
They have gone too far at last. My time has come,
And I can strike them back. Now do you see
Why I have been obsessed with this long struggle?"

The queen, with lowered face, pulled thoughtfully
At the white threads, and finally looked up
And said in quiet tones, "I sometimes think
You would rather prove their oracle was false
Than have me back alive."

                                The king's face whitened.
His hand groped, and he swayed. Looking about,
He found a bench and sat. "That's a hard word,
That's a hard word to come from you, Alcestis."

   The queen went on, speaking more rapidly.
"Just as you say, excess brings its own cure.
Perhaps, if you had been a little gracious
And let them have their story, they would have seen
Their own excess the sooner."

                              "Gracious, you say!
Graciously let them have their offerings
And fatten on choice lambs for a lie's sake!
Graciously let them have their lie itself,
Their story, as you put it! That would be gracious,
It would indeed. It would deliver me
Helpless and bound into their hands forever."

   "But can you blot the story from men's minds
Or keep them from believing it? What harm

In letting those who will take it for true?"

"You are right in one point. This tale will be told
To the world's end. I am helpless to prevent it.
But where's the harm, you say? If I myself
Accede one instant and admit for true
This tale they spread, they have me in their claws
And they will scratch my throne away from me
And turn me to a slave. It's not alone
The stench of bloody sacrifice around us.
You know what they demand. They'd have me go
To Delphi, and there, cringing on my knees,
Babble my gratitude, and thank Apollo—
Thank him for what? For dooming me to die,
And then allowing you to serve instead
The purposes of his divine displeasure,
And then allowing Hercules— The words
Disgust a sane man's mouth! I cannot say them!"

The king sprang up and poured on her bent head
The passion of his thought. "You have no taste
For metaphysical questions. I've held back
From the chief point, Alcestis. Now I ask,
Have you considered what this oracle,
This miracle, should I admit them true,

Would make of me, and since I am a man
Would make through my example of mankind?
All men are cowards, and I am a man,
Therefore a coward, too. Oh, I well know it!
A man, though, can redeem himself. At least
He can struggle with his weakness. I am king,
I can make war and lead my army out
And prove that I am not afraid to die.
But now suppose this oracle were true:
I am a coward by divine decree,
A poltroon by the edict of the gods,
Tricked, with no choice, into receiving life
At my queen's hands! I'll not accept that, never,
No, though I lose my throne! I'll fight it out
Till I have whipped these priests or they have killed me."
    Again Alcestis looked up at her husband.
"When were you ever a coward?"
                              "Oh, I have been!
I have a troubled conscience, and toward you.
Do you remember when Apollodorus
Entered, as I was lying on my couch
That summer afternoon, and first announced
His oracle? With my whole mind, I tell you,

And my whole heart, I never once believed
And never shall and never could believe
Those words of his were anything but fraud. .
Yet when you spoke—I hear your very tone,
So forthright, womanly, and unafraid—
'If the oracle is true'—that's what you said—
'I offer myself—' And as I heard the words,
I felt a little cowardly thrill of safety
From some dark corner of my hidden soul
That told me, 'If it is true, I shall live.'
If I'm a man and have my human will,
Perhaps I can atone for that some day.
But if the gods by trickery determined
That I should serve to all time as the type
And emblem of a poltroon on a throne,
What hope have I? What hope has any man?"

    The queen smiled with a sudden tenderness.
"O poor Admetus! You worry your mind so hard
Over such questions, you make such points of conscience—
Perhaps it has been that—" she said, and stopped.

    "That what?" the king demanded, and the queen
Allowed a deepened and a saddened look
To pass into her face. Her hands grew busy

With hoop and thread a moment, and then fell.

"Sometimes I wonder why it was I lived.
So near to death," she said, "I should have seized
My kindly opportunity, and died."

"Alcestis, God forbid!"

"Oh yes, I know.
You wanted me to live. If I had not,
That would have given the priests their final proof.
It would have shown their oracle was true.
You would have lost your argument, Admetus.
That would have been too much for you to bear."

The king cried out, "You do me an injustice!
Though you had died, I would not have believed
Their lying oracle!"

"I should have died
Rather than come back from the verge of death
Unneeded and unloved."

"What do you mean,
Unloved, Alcestis? How can you say that?"

"You have not come to me since I grew well.
Night after night I hear you pacing about,
Keeping yourself away from me, or thinking,
Or plotting ways to bicker with the priests,

I don't know what."

　　　　　　"How could I tell you wanted—
To me it seemed the other way about.
It seemed that you were cold or even hostile.
And, I'll confess it, I have been unmanned.
I have not been myself. Thanks to these priests
I stand before the court, a king who holds
His own life at the cost of yours, or would,
But for this whimsical feat of Hercules.
When I appeal to reason, I am proud,
Ungrateful, impious, dangerous to the state.
No, I say flatly, I must beat them back
And vindicate myself. That will be soon,
I promise you, and then, Alcestis, then
We can repair all damage we have suffered.
One form of damage will be sweet to heal!
Tonight, Alcestis, when the sun goes down
And the swallows that have newly come again
Go to their nests, tonight we'll love and sleep.
Oh, we'll make damage with the best of them!"

　　The king made toward her with a sudden stride,
His arms reaching ahead as if to seize
And roughen her with hunger. But the queen

Sat silent, bending still above her work,
And awkwardly he balanced and fell back,
Defeated by the stiff clean crust of linen
Heaped in her lap, and by her hands, absorbed
In drawing the white threads. Then she looked up
And said, "Would it really be intolerable
If Hercules had saved me?"

                                 "What do you mean?
You don't believe the tale our priests have fostered
More than I do myself."

                           "Not that, perhaps."

  "Then what?"

                        The queen at last put down her work,
Fixing her needle through the unfinished figure
Traced by the snowy threads, and on a stool
Beside her feet piling it all together.

  "I was thinking of a dream I had."

                              "A dream?"

  "When I was sick. It was a dream so real,
So piercing that I feel it even now.
The sense of it comes back so warm and strange
It seems as though I am living in two worlds
And hardly know to which one I belong."

"What did you dream?"

                              Alcestis for a moment
Studied him apprehensively, then smiled
And said in her distinct and gentle voice,
"I dreamed that Hercules rescued me from death."

    Admetus quivered, turned round with bent shoulders,
And sat down on his bench. "Now what, Alcestis?
What do you mean to do? Extract from dreams
New portents and new evidence against me?
If an old woman's hen so much as lays
An egg with two yolks, it becomes a portent,
A supernatural sign foreboding woe,
An omen to the state. You tell me now
You dreamed that Hercules saved you. What of that?"

    "I don't know what. I thought perhaps that you,
With all your mind for metaphysical questions,
Could tell me what."

                       "But what is there to tell?
I see no more in this odd dream of yours
Than still another link in the strange chain
Coincidence has twisted round our court.
It's lucky that our priests, who have their ears
In the wall of every room, can't pry their way

Into your dreams. What an oracular net
They would have made of this to snare me in!"

The queen sighed. "Then it means no more," she said,
"Than just a word, coincidence. To you
It means no more."

                              "Tell me your dream, Alcestis,"
The king demanded. "Tell me the whole of it,
All you remember, to the least shade and scrap."

"I was going on a journey," said the queen.
"I had promised you to go, and yet it seemed
You had deserted me. You would not come
When I called out. You would not give me help."

"Ah, that reproach is too just," said the king.
"My weakness rises up on your behalf
To call it true. Forgive me, if you can!"

"The way was dark and waste, and at my back
Some horrible creature prowled. Then I turned round
And he was tall and fair, a god, I thought.
He said that he had come to be my guide.
He made me promises and flattered me.
I did not know how I could keep my pledge
Unless I went with him, and yet it seemed
I could not go and yet be faithful too.

I yielded to him once. He offered rest,
And I was tired. But then I fought and screamed,
And he leaped on me with a horrible face
In which snakes crawled and crumbled. Then I heard
The voice and feet of Hercules running to help me,
And suddenly he was there. He rescued me
By his great strength. It was the strangest dream!
I can remember it still so vividly
It spins me in a thick cocoon of sleep
That seems more living than the midday sun."

   "Truly a strange dream, truly profound and strange,"
The king said slowly. "I do not wonder at all
That my poor word 'coincidence' falls lame
When set beside a dream so apt as this.
If we could only know when it took place—"

   "My waiting women tell me," said Alcestis,
"That just before the fever left my forehead,
Or cooled a little, I tossed and fought the bedclothes
And groaned thick words as though clenched in a nightmare,
And then lay still, and from that hour, they say,
I steadily got better."

              "What, the moment,
The very moment when our drunken hero

Roared through the court with such a tide of sound
It might have washed the shores of death itself!
Do you suppose the rough edge of his din
Broke through your sleep, and reached you, lying there
At the very point of death? Do you suppose—"

The king broke off, hearing behind his back
A sound of interruption. He swung about,
And in the doorway stood Eugenius,
His counselor.

                    "Pardon," the old man said.
"I come on pressing missions, two at once."
He bowed. The king said patiently, "What are they?"
"Hercules has arrived," Eugenius told him.
"Here? Now? Himself? Are you sure?" the king demanded.
"He is not a man one easily mistakes,"
Eugenius answered, smiling. "He is here,
No doubt of it. He's being washed and dined."
Admetus rallied. "Give him every welcome,
Extend him every courtesy. You have,
I know; you do not need directions for it.
But at this crux in our affairs—we'll see him
As soon as he is ready." Admetus laughed.
"Hercules! Now, Alcestis, you shall see

Your rescuer in person, not, this time,
So far gone in his cups, I hope!"
                                    The queen
Looked quietly up and said, "Please do not mock him."
    "You do not know how seriously I speak,"
Admetus answered. "Now for your second mission.
What's that, Eugenius?"
                            "One I tried to spare you.
Apollodorus waits outside, demanding—
Yes, that's the word—to speak with you at once.
I tried to put him off, but he's wrought up
To such a pitch by the orders you have given—"
    "I am not surprised. Well, I'll not stand on form.
Let him come in, yes, here and now, Eugenius."
    The counselor bowed and went to usher in
The waiting priest. The king turned to Alcestis.
"My medicine begins to work," he said.
"Now we shall learn, sooner than I expected,
What its effects will be."
                            "More bitterness,
More bickering? I hope not," said the queen.
    "This is no petty quarrel," the king answered.
"I'll try to keep it above pettiness,

But I shall never yield. I stand on that."

The tall priest pushed Eugenius aside
And shouldered through the door. The old counselor
Followed him with offended dignity.
Apollodorus took a threatening posture
Before the king, and with his fleshy eyes
Black and unblinking looked down at his foe.

"I charge you by the god I serve, proud king,
With new impieties."

                   Admetus trembled,
Controlled himself, and smiled. "I have no ear
For such a charge. If you have any business
Or any true complaint that I can answer,
State the particulars."

                      "You have overruled
And countermanded the appeasing rites
And special offerings that we, the priests—"

Admetus raised his arm. "So I have done,
And I confirm my order, here and now.
No special sacrifice, from this time on,
By my own edict, shall be held again—"

Eugenius coughed. "May I suggest," he said,
"That if you both, in private, should sit down

And should consult, the king with his own conscience
And you, Apollodorus, with the help
Of priestly auguries and auspices,
It might appear the gods would be content
With some wise mean or compromise between you."
　　The king smiled. "What, negotiate with the gods?
No, my old friend, I'll have no compromise.
You both know what I think. Your oracle,
Apollodorus, was to me a lie
From the first moment that you uttered it.
And you would not be here accusing me
Unless you knew you had overshot your mark.
Take yourself out among the huts and pastures,
Try to reverse my edict if you can!
I tell you, priest, the shepherds and the herdsmen
Have seen you stuff yourselves on mutton and beef
Until they would have hidden their flocks away
In the wild creases of the farthest hills
Had I not ordered these unholy rites
To stop forthwith. Oh, you have plowed their minds
With superstitious fear, but they can tell,
In time, the luxury of a priest's gullet
From a god's anger!"

"You refuse to go

In pilgrimage to Delphi, there to pay

Your debt of gratitude—"

"I do refuse,"

The king said. "Who would rule while I am gone?"

"A regency could be arranged, Admetus,"

Eugenius told him.

"A regency of priests!

No, I refuse, and there's an end to that."

"You have thrown my priests in prison!"

"Two of your caste

Who went about seducing the court girls,

Or trying to, made reckless by the wine

You poured out in libations to the gods!

I have them in detention, true enough,

And there I mean to keep them till they learn

Some self-restraint."

Apollodorus turned,

And his black gaze fixed suddenly on Alcestis.

"Queen, whom Apollo has seen fit to save,

Faithful Alcestis, once more save your husband,

Over whose kingdom hangs the appointed vengeance

That waits upon impiety!"

"Now, priest,
You have reached the summit of your villainy!
You'd sow dissension between man and wife,
Scheme for a woman's aid—"

                "Oh, spare yourselves
From quarreling over me," Alcestis told them.
"Let the gods do with me as the gods will.
My husband's fate is mine."

            "Then I forsake
This kingdom and its doom," the priest declared
With stiff, impassive face. "I do not need
To curse this realm of Thessaly. A curse
Hangs over it in the dread brows of the gods.
I shall not wait to see the shadow fall
Nor learn what prodigy groans in the bowels of earth
To issue forth and ravage a lost land."

   He turned and strode out. The king shrugged and laughed.
   "There goes your oracle, Eugenius! Mark,
It walks on two conniving human legs.
Has he really gone? Is it over, and so quickly?"

   "You have triumphed, King Admetus. At what cost
Who knows? May it never prove an evil omen."

   "The world is never free from grief, old friend.

It does not need an omen to bring on
The chances and the strokes of human life.
But now go see that everything is done
For the comfort of our hero, Hercules."
  Admetus let the old man reach the door
And then turned to Alcestis. "I have curbed
Their priestly impudence at last," he said.
"We are well rid of him. Now I rule again,
I am master of my household and myself.
But through this altercation, half my mind
Has been possessed by that strange dream of yours.
Do you know what I am coming to believe?
I think your dream was true—not in the way
The priests would have it. No, you clung to life,
You would not die, Alcestis. When the scales
Dipped on the fulcrum, when the rough knee of death
Was on your breast, you called on your own strength,
The common, vulgar tie that binds us all
To our brief share of light. That rescued you,
That saved and brought you back to us, Alcestis!
But how should it appear to you in dream,
What tangible shape could it assume so well
As Hercules, the demigod of strength,

The very form and symbol of vulgar force?
And so it did, so it was he indeed
Who saved you. Hercules offered the guise
In which your own indomitable will
Could find embodiment. Yet, I hardly know!
I feel a deeper mystery. Could it have been
That the great drunken blast of sound he vented
When he went roaring through the passageway
Reached you, and gave you at the fatal instant
A clue to seize, an image in your dream,
Without which you might never have found the strength
To thwart your dark antagonist? If so,
He saved you in a sense more literal still.
I have made much of reason, but, Alcestis,
I do not lack a sense of mystery.
If but for blundering Hercules and his drink
You would have died, then in all truth he came
As mystery's agent. Who can say at last
By whom or what our lives are shaped? For me
Mystery is still mystery. Riches and terror
Lie in its keeping. We profane it merely
When we assert we know its oracles,
When we expound its laws as if we sat

In the center and dark source of the world's will.
It is not mystery that I reject
But men's ways of explaining mystery,
By which they make themselves puppets and slaves
To their own superstition. This I say:
Gladly I'll owe your life to Hercules,
However this great feat of his was done."

 The queen sat listening thoughtfully, her face
Withdrawn but not displeased. At length she said,
"That wasn't all my dream. The strangest part
I haven't told you yet."

      "Tell me, Alcestis."

 "When Hercules had saved me, the queer part—
How shall I say it? I needed all his strength,
That's how I felt. I wanted to reward him,
And you were far away, I could not find you.
I offered him— I laugh when I remember!
He wouldn't have me, it put him in a fright!"

 "Hercules frightened!" The king laughed in his turn.
"And of an offer such as that! Go on."

 "There's little more. In a short time I felt
That Hercules didn't matter. He slipped off
Almost as if I had myself dismissed him,

And then I knew I should be well again,
Knew that I'd wake, as a child wakes from nightmare."
   "Strange and profound, profound and strange, Alcestis!
But now, since I have played interpreter,
Let me interpret further, if I can.
You needed all the common and crude strength
By which, past reason, we hold fast to life,
And found that strength in Hercules, and used it.
But once used, what could you, a lovely woman,
Do with such male force, turbulent and blind?
Unite with it completely? No, Alcestis,
It would have crushed you, even as Hercules
Crushed Deianeira. Always the truest natures
Have in them something of both woman and man,
But let the balance tip on either side,
Too much of man in woman or woman in man,
And then we have nature's perversities.
This is an allegory, this dream of yours!
All these events that we have suffered here
Begin to show their meaning in your dream.
Whether the author of the allegory
Was life or chance or some designing god,
That is the mystery!"

"In the dream itself
It seemed as though he spoke of Deianeira,"
The queen said wonderingly.

                    "I'm not surprised
That he was frightened, that he would not have you,
Or you dismissed him when his gift of strength
Had done its work. All these were intuitions
You carried over from a woman's knowledge
Into your dream."

                    "When he comes in, Admetus,
Ask him about that night."

                    "He was not there
In person with you, walking the wastes of sleep.
All this was in your mind."

                    "Ask him, Admetus,
If only to please me."

                    "Of course I will,"
Promised the king. "I'll ask whatever you like.
But if you think—"

                    Then in the corridor
They heard a soft gigantic pad of feet.
Admetus turned, Alcestis rose and stood,
And in the door the great scruffed head appeared,

The black and staring eyes, the bristled limbs
And huge trunk newly clad in a fresh tunic,
A size of man that beggared memory
And racked the eyes for a new scale of vision
Each time he was perceived.

"Welcome, good friend,"
Admetus cried, and Hercules advanced,
Genial and beaming.

"I see a lot has changed
Since I was here last time. You're well again.
The gods have made you twice as beautiful
After that fever you went through, Queen Alcestis."
  "Now that's as pretty a speech as ever I heard!
Thank you," Alcestis told him.

The king smiled.
"The gods, I think, did less than you yourself
To give Alcestis back to us," he said.
"But we'll talk later about that. Sit down,
We'll speak at leisure."

He found and pulled up benches,
And the queen sat beside her work again.
"The children, are they well, too?" asked the hero.
  "Shouting and scuffling all day long," the queen said.

"The boys must thank you for that colt you brought
When you came back from Thrace."

                                  Hercules winked.

"Hasn't eaten 'em up yet?"

                              "Not one nip."

  "They'll make a warhorse of him, give them time.
I'd show them how to drive a chariot
If I could stay awhile, but King Eurystheus
Has given me another job to do.
I'm on the road again." Hercules paused
And looked about. "Your royal father and mother,
Admetus, aren't they here?"

                          "In our long siege
With death and winter, it was they who died,"
Answered the king.

                 "Well now, I didn't know,"
Said Hercules gruffly. "Your father was a hunter.
Told me himself once how he shot a lion.
I had a present for him, tusk of a boar
I killed along the way, big as the one
I killed that time up on Mount Erymanthus."

  "It would have been the pride of his last days
To take it from your hands, but he is gone."

"Likely enough they went in their own time,"
Said Hercules. "Age is the time to go.
Soon as a man can't hunt or do the things
He used to do, can't see, can't hear—I say
It's best to cut the mooring and ship off."

"Even so," the king said. "But Alcestis, too,
Came very near to death. Now she's restored,
And we have every reason, Hercules,
To thank you for it. The crisis in her fever
Fell on that very night when you were here
During the winter. Do you recall that night?"

"I remember things were in a bad way then,"
Hercules answered, knotting up his face
With intellectual effort. "Ambassadors
Kept coming in and out, making excuses,
Throwing the gibblegabble thick and fast—
Never did find out what was going on."

"Do you remember that I came myself
To say we thought Alcestis all but dead?
Do you remember that you seized my neck
And tried to make me lead you to her room?"

"Did I do that? Did I grab you by the neck?
I shouldn't have done that!" The hero's jaw

Fell down abashed.

                "It doesn't matter at all,
Not in the least," the king said hastily.
"Tell us what you remember of that night.
You understand our eagerness, good friend.
That was the night when, after every hope
Showed us its back and scurried down the road
Away from Thessaly, Alcestis turned
From death to life."

                Hercules looked about
As if he sought escape. "I never was much
At recollection," he said uncomfortably.
"I tell you how it was. I got in cold,
Maybe I'd covered fifty, sixty miles
That day, driving those mares along from Thrace.
My appetite was up, and I was thirsty,
And there was food and good wine on the table,
Not like the slops they give me in Mycenae.
What with the heat inside, and all those people,
Ambassadors and poets coming and going,
Gabbing out riddles I couldn't understand,
I guess the wine went to my head a little.
You know how it is after a night like that—

· 113 ·

You can't remember anything at all.
You have to find out later what you did
From someone else, just as you told me now
About the way I grabbed you by the neck.
I shouldn't have done that!"

                             "Forgive me, friend,
For troubling you with questions," the king said.
"The truth is, I believe you saved Alcestis.
Do you know she dreamed of you, at the very time,
It well may be, when—pardon, Hercules!—
You bellowed you would drive death from her door?
And so you would have done, I know, if death
Had been a thief in solid flesh and blood,
A monster to be strangled by your hands.
But as it was, you lent your gift of strength
Unknowingly, but when her need was greatest.
Remember that, whatever you may hear,
Wherever you go. Remember for my sake!"

   The hero gaped and shook his head bewildered.
"She dreamed, you say? Alcestis dreamed of me?"
He beamed with comical pleasure. "And she lived?
I like to think of that! It might have killed her,
A face like mine, and in a lady's dream!"

"I never have seen a face or friend more welcome,"
The queen said with a smile, "sleeping or waking."

"Well now, that's one I never heard the like of
Since they turned me to a goosegirl in Mycenae.
If I were going to dream, I'd rather see
A crocodile, if that's the thing I mean.
I've seen 'em, anyway, down there in Egypt,
In the river Nile."

              "You have traveled to the world's end!
Where are you going now, and what new task
Have you embarked on?" asked the queen.

                      "Up north,

Over a piece of road I never tramped
Until I got this job. Seems there's a flock,
The oddest fowl I ever heard about,
They call 'em the Stymphalian birds. They nest
Thicker than grasshoppers in a plague year
And squawk and jabber the whole day and night.
They say it's worse than a thousand axes grinding,
And what with all the droppings and the noise
People can't sleep or live in decent comfort.
I've got to drive them off."

                "There's no mistake?"

Admetus asked. "These birds aren't feathered priests?"

"Real birds," Hercules answered seriously,
"By all I'm told. I hear they have brass feathers.
I'll pick one up and bring it to the children
If you'd like it as a thing to have around.
Don't let that fever come back while I'm gone!"

The hero rose. The king said, "Hercules,
You will not leave us now? The day is late.
Stay with us and we'll celebrate tonight.
We'll banquet and we'll have the dancers in.
We've much to thank you for. Alcestis lives.
And Thessaly begins to swim again
In the current of her old and natural life."

"No telling what I'd do," Hercules answered.
"I wouldn't want to grab you by the neck
Another time! Besides, I have this job.
I can't rest till I do it. Work, that's for me.
I'm safest when I'm carrying out my orders.
I'll find my way by star as well as sunlight.
There's many a stretch of road I've tramped by night
Over the mountains, hearing the wolves bay
And the winds wail around the peaks and caverns.
I'll go, Admetus."

"And my gratitude

Go with you everywhere," Admetus answered.

   "Lady Alcestis, anything I can do,

Some little service any time at all,

Just let me know."

                "Come back to Thessaly,"

The queen said, and they stood to watch him go.

   He filled the columned entrance as he passed,

The lion of Cithaeron rippling down

Over his tunic to his knees behind him,

Its eyeless head fastened beneath his neck,

Its claws on either side, as though the beast

Had just sprung and was hanging there transfixed

In a perpetual, blinded desperation.

Then he had vanished, and Admetus turned

To face Alcestis.

                "Are you disappointed?"

"Oh, no, how could I be?" Alcestis laughed

A little ruefully. "What I expected

I can't imagine! But poor Hercules!

We must be kind to him. He needs much kindness."

   "We shall be, both of us. You have the gift

Of kindness more than I, but I shall learn.

Will you be kind to me again, Alcestis?"

"You ask as though I had not been," she said.

"Rather as though I need much kindness, too.
Oh, I can see myself in the same light
As you and all my court have viewed me in!
I see the ignoble figure I have cut.
I have seemed selfish, I have seemed obsessed
With my own battle, though at heart believing
I fought for all men, if they only knew it!
I have seemed arrogant and ungrateful. Yes,
The very charge that scheming priest of ours
Brought on my head has been in some part true,
For all that in his mouth it was a web
Of lies and fraud! I have seemed callous, blind
To the graces that you wear in the world's eye,
Blind to the sacrifice you would have made—
Faithful Alcestis!"

      "I am not a saint,"
The queen said vehemently. "I am a woman.
I did not think of sacrifice. I spoke
As an impulsive girl. I did not know
What I should suffer."

      "You must be content

With your perfections, even as I must be
With all my imperfections. Neither of us
Believed the oracle, but for all that
You said the words you said. You have been brushed
By sacred wings, if any wings are sacred,
The wings of sorrow and of sacrifice.
You stand above me in men's eyes. With that
I am happy enough. But this is what I ask:
Have I won my battle with the priests, Alcestis,
My necessary fight that I shall never
Repent of fighting nor repent of winning,
Have I hacked out in the tangle of superstition
A tiny clearing where I may stand up,
Though few should join me there, only to lose—"
The king's breath shook and strained. "Or will you have me,
Have me for what I am, for what I must be?"

    The walls and the trim columns of the court
Slept in the clear light while his question waited.
Then, woman indeed, and ready to be taken,
She said, "Why else did I come back from death?"

DATE DUE

#47-0108 Peel Off Pressure Sensitive